This Little Tiger book belongs to:

_____

_____

_____

In memory of Lorraine
~ S. C.
For Jane and Tim
~ S. P.

LITTLE TIGER PRESS
1 The Coda Centre,
189 Munster Road, London SW6 6AW
www.littletiger.co.uk

First published in Great Britain 1999
by Little Tiger Press, London
This edition published 2012

Printed in China • LTP/1900/0835/0913

2 4 6 8 10 9 7 5 3

GOODNIGHT, LITTLE HARE

Sheridan Cain
Sally Percy

LITTLE TIGER PRESS

By the pale light of the moon, Mother Hare
sat watching Little Hare. He lay with eyes tightly
shut. For his blanket he had the sky, and the
soft hay formed his bed.

"Goodnight, Little Hare," she whispered.

Mole trundled by and almost toppled over Little Hare.
"Mother Hare," he said, "you cannot leave your baby there.
It isn't safe, for the farmer cuts the hay at dawn."

"But what can I do?" asked Mother Hare. "Where can
Little Hare sleep?"

"You should dig a hole, big and deep," said Mole.
"That's where your little baby should sleep."

So Mother Hare began to dig.

She scraped and scraped
at the soft, brown earth, until
the hole was big and deep. Then
she carried Little Hare to his new bed.

But Little Hare did not like it. "Mama," he cried. "It's so dark and I'm afraid."

Badger came bumbling along and heard
Little Hare's cry. "Mother Hare," he said,
"you cannot leave your baby there. It isn't safe.
Weasel is hunting through hole and burrow,
and he will soon find Little Hare."

"But what can I do?" asked Mother Hare.
"Where can Little Hare sleep?"
"You should cover him in a bed of
leaves. That will fool Weasel,"
said Badger.

So Mother Hare
hurried and scurried.

She formed the leaves
into a soft, round pile.
Then she carried Little Hare
to his new bed.

But Little Hare did not like it. "Mama,"
he cried. "I'm so afraid. I don't like the crinkly,
crackly noise my new bed makes."

Blackbird was up early, pecking among the
leaves for grubs when he heard Little Hare's cry.
 "Mother Hare," he said, "you cannot leave your
baby there. It isn't safe. Fox's nose is sharp
and he will soon sniff out Little Hare."
 "But what can I do?" asked Mother Hare.
 "Where can Little Hare sleep?"
 "What you need is a nest
 up high," said Blackbird.
 "Fox will never reach
 him there."

So Mother Hare leaped up
onto the branch of a tree
and placed Little Hare
in an empty bird's nest.

But Little Hare did not like it.
"Mama," he cried, looking down.
"I'm so afraid. It's high up here
and I might fall out."

Mother Hare carried Little Hare down
again. She did not know what to do.
"Oh, dear," she sobbed. "How can I
find a bed that's safe for Little Hare?"

Owl was watching
Mother Hare and Little
Hare from his perch.

"Don't be sad," said Owl.
"Don't you remember when *you*
were young and how *your* mother
kept you safe?"

Mother Hare remembered the sky
that was her blanket. She remembered
the soft, golden hay that was her bed.

She remembered how, from
dusk to dawn, her mother
had watched over her.

The sun was just rising.
Mother Hare looked toward
the field that was her home,
and her eyes became bright.
The farmer had come early
and the hay was cut.

It was safe there now.

Mother Hare carried
Little Hare back to his
old bed and laid him
gently down.

"Mama," said Little Hare.
"I'm not afraid now. This is
my own bed and I like it."

Goodnight, Little Hare!